D R A U G R

Gunnhild Lashtongue Series
Book One

First Published in Great Britain 2016 by Mirador Publishing

First edition: 2016
Second edition: 2017

ISBN: 978-1-911473-64-0

Mirador Publishing
10 Greenbrook Terrace
Taunton
Somerset
TA1 1UT
UK

Draugr

Gunnhild Lashtongue Series
Book One

By

Geoff Hill

Also by the author

Gunnhild Lashtongue Series:
Draugr
Bäckahäst
Huldra

For all matters related to the Gunnhild Lashtongue
series, visit Geoff Hill's Amazon Author Page.
Or find us on Facebook.
Please leave a review to let us know what you think.
Royalties from all sales go to St Pauls School,
Chippenham, Wilts.

Dedicated to my dad

William John Finch Hill

*who taught me to love stories
and that life goes on.*

Chapter One

Leif Haraldson was getting too old for this.

He felt the cold gnawing at his bones; he shook, coughing wretchedly in the chilly air; he heard the creak in his back like a straining branch under a fall of snow. Sea-frost crusted his eyebrows and beard, and an ache of weariness sank into his goatskin boots. Pretending to stretch his mighty shoulders, he cast a swift glance across the fjord.

A little way behind Haraldson's ragged crew of pirates crouched Gunnhild Lashtongue, softly and silently blending with the treeline and drifting snow. Her thin face was striped with charcoal like a mountain tiger, her fur cloak pulled tight around her throat. She had followed the warriors for nearly three exhausting days and nights now, like a grey shadow in the silver woods. She might have been cold and hungry and tired, but her fierce pride would never let it show.

"Still she haunts us!" whispered Sven Bjørnson.

Leif grunted. Sven had covered his mouth with a grubby hand – that way, the girl would not see his lips move – but Leif could still hear the shiver in his warrior's voice.

Bjørnson wore a wolf-skin with the mouth stretched wide and snarling around his grizzled head: the mark of an *Úlfhédnar*: a Berserker. He had sailed with Haraldson's crew for longer than any of them remembered, the strongest and most ferocious of all.

Haraldson could plot their route as if marked on a chart on his parchment forehead: from Kaupang, Strandebarm and Frøya, across seas steep-backed like mountains; through storms of furious wind and knife-edged hail to the coast of Angland; over sea-ice packed like granite, into the sunless night of Svalbard.

Together they had ransacked the monastery on Lindesfarne, plundered warehouses in Jorvik, and explored the bleak and dismal coast of Greenland. If Bjørnson the Berserker had a shiver in his voice, what good would be the rest of the men?

"We are close now," muttered the old jarl to his cut-throat crew.

***

The great long-hall of Eirik Blacktooth rose looming from the fog, like a monster from the deep. In years gone by, it had been *Torwurm*, the king's long-ship, which had prowled the coast and savaged the seas until the time came for Eirik to settle, dragging the huge hull up the stony beach and upturning it to make the roof over a vast oval of piled rock: his hull became his great hall. In the gloom, it lay glaring and gaunt, wet with sleet and sagging with rot.

With their skin prickling from more than just the cold, the Vikings stepped warily over the threshold, into the inky blackness of the deserted hall. Their arrows were nocked, swords raised, axes poised…

Not a soul stirred in the place. The hearth fire had long since perished. The congealed remains of some suspect stew swam in the cauldron. Dust and bird droppings caked the floor-planks.

The men began to mutter and Haraldson saw he had to stamp this out – this cold fire of fear would spread and destroy their nerve. He growled his orders, sending scouts to sweep the clearing and report back to him when they had found any trace of Blacktooth's people.

"After all, they won't be far in this weather, hey?"

The joke spilt in the echoes of the hall, weak and flat like watered beer, so he went back to scowling at them. This, they seemed to almost prefer. Hefting their weapons, they slunk back out into the bitter ever-night, rasping and wheezing with every breath.

At least they took their stench with them, thought the jarl: their sour reek of sweat, their constant itch of fleas, their endless moaning. For the last few weeks they had bleated about pine needles in their feet or of feeling too leaden with fatigue to stand.

Heaving his fearsome battle-axe *Heart-Halver* from the harness across his back, Haraldson chopped a carved chair into kindling and set about striking a fire, using flints and a little dry wool he kept in a seal-skin pouch.

His shoulder ached cruelly again. While the fire woke sleepily in the hearth, he took off his tattered gauntlets to explore the sore and angry scar that ran from armpit to collarbone. He sighed – and immediately had to fight off another mob of coughs. The wound was taking a devil of a time to heal. At least the movement seemed easier, even if the cut smelled worse than his men.

They were taking longer than he would have expected.

Grumbling, he strode to the door and peered out into the swirling snow. The light of the sun was barely clinging to the horizon, far out beyond the grey surf and rolling icebergs. Winter had seized the land in icy jaws and shaken the life from it.

Haraldson had sailed this far north before: he knew how the sun withered and died up here at the roof of the world, leaving only a line of blood where the sea swallowed the sky.

Out of the infinite dark came his Vikings, plodding and slipping on the ice and mossy rocks. Carefully, he counted them back into the hall, like a shepherd with his flock, looking for any news in their haggard faces… but all were silent and grim.

Without a word, they gathered round the weak fire and pleaded with it for warmth. The giant sea-captain frowned.

Januld the Walrus had not returned.

"Ach!" spat Sven Bjørnson when Haraldson pointed it out, "That fat lump could never keep up!"

"Maybe he is lost in the dark?" suggested another of the crew, a rat-faced Icelander called Torstein.

"Maybe you'd best find him then," grunted Haraldson.

In the firelight, the jarl's eyes burned with a fury.

Torstein sighed and struggled to his feet again with a wet, hacking cough, glancing miserably around him for a companion.

"Pieter Magnussen, you'll come to watch my back?"

Magnussen was a tall, lean Swede with a long white moustache and a temper as sour as his smell.

"Ach! Watch your own back!" he grumbled.

Still Torstein dawdled in the doorway, until at last Bjørnson the berserker threw a boot at his head. With a petulant curse upon all their heads, the miserable man stumbled off into the dark again. In a short while, they could hear him calling for Januld the Walrus, using a rich and violent variety of adjectives.

Bjørnson began pulling pine needles from his blackened feet, muttering dark curses of his own. There were no songs or stories around the fire. The Vikings drew up their cloaks and slept upright, leaning back to back for warmth and protection.

It was to be a long night – the longest they'd known.

***

With the stealth of a great cat, Gunnhild Lashtongue crept through the lower branches. Pines clung to the pitiless slopes of the fjord, like an army of spears stabbing through the snowdrifts. In her white furs, she was all but invisible.

Blacktooth's long-hall, however, lay sprawled across a clearing at the top of the pebbled beach; a naked flat stretch of sea-grass and rocks, with no cover in which to lurk unseen. Reaching a skeletal hand into her jerkin, the little witch brought out fistfuls of sooty paste and smeared it through her wild hair and across her feral face.

With a shrug of her bony shoulders, she flipped the fur cloak inside-out to reveal a night-black lining; then she began ripping tufts of sea-grass out of the rock and stuffing them through slits in the cloth. All the while, she kept a keen eye on the dying sun as it bled to death over the icy sea. Patiently, she waited for the pale, goose grey of the day to give way to the murky, cormorant black of the ever-night.

When the murder of light was almost over, she began to crawl on all claws from the shadows of the treeline, over the tufted rock; her icy eyes glimmering in their coal-black sockets, her vicious knife glinting between her sharpened teeth.

She found exactly the right spot – just where the sea-grass met the pebbled slope to the beach. Laying out dank and slimy strands of sea-weed across the rocks, she whispered a kenning-spell over them and then drew back into the shadows, fixing a gull-feathered arrow to her bowstring.

She did not need to wait for long.

The one they called Januld the Walrus was puffing across the clearing towards her.

The sinew bowstring was pulled to her cracked lips; over the slender arrow, she whispered another kenning: "Skull-Ringer!"

– then, let fly.

***

Haraldson rolled in his sleep, plunging through the icy waves, holding fast to the tiller and roaring over the winds as he fought to keep the prow straight and his course true.

His crew scampered like rats across the pitching deck, hauling in the shreds of sail while the bone-numbing water smashed over the side and sent them skidding.

Like a great shaggy hound, he shook the spray from his furs and cursed them all. Heads like goats. If only they had the feet to match.

He had built the long-ship himself in the forests of Strandebarm, where the firs and spruce spread like a green blanket over the mountains. With his own hands, he'd hewn down the timber, warped the planks to shape and nailed each strake and rib to the keel-bone, before planting the mast. The sails had come from Frøya in the north, where the sheep grew the thickest coats of toughest wool, woven on giant looms by cackling teams of women.

The figurehead had been carved in Kaupang by a craftsman from the steppe-lands far to the east. When it was brought to the village, the men had left it outside the gates.

No-one else would touch it.

The moment he saw it was the moment Leif Haraldson finally found the name for his ship: *Linnorm*. It was a monster of grotesquery, fanged and gilled, scaled and horned. As it was hoisted and fastened to the prow, the men swore it looked down upon them with a nictating eye. The sea-captain felt a strange thrill.

When the first flowers began to push through the snow, the Vikings had thrown their great sea-chests aboard and sat at the oars, hanging their shields over the sides and singing cheerfully as the tide took them away.

The ship of his slumber rolled Haraldson roughly back and he glimpsed again, through the blinding lightning and flashing spray, the Linnorm uncoiling from the prow, turning back upon them through the storm, her fangs raging wide, her eyes hissing green…

Haraldson woke to find the ravens pecking at his legs again and slapped them off with a mutter. He never really slept any more.

Sven Bjørnson came to say that they'd found the Walrus.

"Good!" grinned Haraldson; then he looked again at the berserker's face and saw it wasn't.

***

Januld the Walrus lay on a patch of seaweed, his skull split open on a rock and his brains seeping into the pebbles.

"Idiot must've slipped over in the dark," Haraldson drawled, not even bothering to draw closer.

However, his wolf-furred lieutenant was crouching over the frozen corpse, tapping his fingertips together as he always did when thinking hard.

"This sea-weed was placed here," he swept a hand across the landscape, "There's no more like it this far up the beach."

"Ach!" grouched the captain, "The winds would've blown it in the night – not that you could really call this, *day*."

The grey light was feebler than yesterday. There would be only a few hours of that… before the dark returned.

Still the wolf-man examined Januld's body, now blue with cold and death.

"Then where is his helmet?"

"He lost it in the storm!" Haraldson snapped, "You look for it if you want."

Painfully, he turned back to the long-hall. Now he was going to have to struggle up the fjord again. Behind him, Bjørnson was rising to his feet and scrambling after. He didn't want to be left out here alone.

"What should we do with his body?"

Haraldson stopped and shrugged. "I don't care anymore. Dig him a grave, build him a barrow – Hel, build him a ship to burn him in, hey?"

Just as he was setting off once more, the Úlfhédnar's next words sank like teeth into his ribs: "We need food."

The great captain's shoulders sagged. Very quietly, he hooked a thumb over his shoulder at the cadaver. "Well, I'm not eating that."

"No," agreed Bjørnson, "But some of the others will want to."

Haraldson could see he was right. He just couldn't see

what to do next, as if he were snow-blind, stumbling through a blizzard.

"Maybe they should," he grunted.

"If we leave him here, the smell will bring bears."

Haraldson grimaced. There was no arguing with that. "But he weighs a ton!"

The wolfman shrugged. "We could cut him up and carry him in pieces."

But when they turned back to the body… it seemed that someone else already had. His head was now missing.

***

Gunnhild Lashtongue lay flat amongst the sea-grass, her deadly eyes trained on the fat Viking now outlined against the charcoal sky. His helmet was a bad fit – he'd stolen it from the dead. The bewitched arrow clanged against the side, sending it spinning off into the dark.

Januld the Walrus knew the *thwip* of an arrow well and bolted back up the beach, his mouth ready to call alarm – but his worn boots betrayed him on the seaweed-slicked rocks and he slipped, toppling backwards with a crack and a squelch.

Letting out a delighted hoot, the little soot-black witch swarmed out of the shadows and sat happily on the dying Viking's chest, warming herself as he cooled.

From the depths of her fur cloak, she drew the shark-tooth knife and cast more magic with his blood and hair, enchanting the blade so that it would reach his *hugr* – his soul. She was preparing to make the cut when the angry voice of another Viking echoed across the clearing. They were looking for him.

With a fierce snarl, Gunnhild shrank back amongst the sea-grass and faded into the night. It couldn't be helped: she would have to come back for his head later.

At least she had the helmet. It was a fine one: riveted iron plates; leather bindings and ties for the cheek plates; skirted with mail down the neck. Best of all, there was a visor to shield the eyes, forged like a metal beak.

In the grey morning, she watched the captain and his wolf-man come down to the beach, arguing over the body, and suddenly it had seemed to her better this way. The risk was worth it.

When they began to trudge back to the long-hall, she stole forward and hacked off the head of Januld the Walrus. They never heard a sound. She lay hidden in the sea-grass, giggling like a little girl, listening to the Vikings' descent into chaos and uproar.

As night fell, she dodged her way back through the forest to the barrow-mound and ate. She took a small lump of white, chalky metal – soft like goat's cheese – and carefully ground it to powder, wrapped it in little packets and tied them to her arrow heads.

"Soul-Scorcher!" she named them, in murmurs.

She tested her traps among the trees; checked the woven twigs which concealed her stake-pits; bent saplings to the ground and secured them.

Climbing back into the branches, she hung noose-snares from the strongest ones and balanced logs in the highest forks.

Finally, back amongst the gloomy stones of the barrow, she cast the runes – the little carved bones that would tell her what to do next.

***

"Now do you believe me?" Bjørnson gasped, "I tell you, she's a *Draugr*, sent from Hel to torment us!"

"Ach!" growled Haraldson, "You're getting to sound like my Great-Aunt Greta! There's no such thing as a Draugr!"

The wolf-man was about to argue again but Haraldson stared him down, his lips curling beneath his filthy moustache. This was not the time to debate the matter. Together, they drew their weapons and stood back to back: each would be the eyes in the back of the other's head.

They stared into the gloom, alert to any movement, but the wind was twisting the snow into blindfolds. Beyond that, the current nudged the sea-ice in an undulating mess of greyness. They might as well have been hunting a snowflake.

Leaving their dead shipmate for the now, they retreated towards the long-hall, all the while keeping one eye on their footing for seaweed. Bjørnson was sprightlier than his old captain and kept trying to force the pace but Haraldson was a boulder that would only roll slowly.

The wolf-man began to harbour dark thoughts. He could smell fear on the jarl: Haraldson knew more than he was letting on. Somehow, he knew this Draugr; this hidden menace that had harried them, hounded them from the first night of the shipwreck, through the freezing trek across the island, finally to Blacktooth's hall.

Who was she?

What did she want with them?

When would the daylight return?

Where were Blacktooth and his people?

How were they going to get off this island?

He felt an avalanche of questions in his weary head and knew he was sliding into terror. He needed more brew.

Ulfgang and Rolf would need it too by now.

There they were, hunkered down, twitching and sniffling by the battered palisade fence that ringed the hall. The moment they caught sight of their brother and the captain crouching in battle-stance, they sprang to their side and, without a word, widened the defensive circle.

They arrived at the great doors, shaken but unharmed.

Gruffly, Haraldson outlined the situation with Januld's body. Something had taken his head while their backs were turned. There were gasps, swiftly covered by prolific profanities. Guards were posted by each door. Soon though, a few joked that at least there would be more food to go round.

"No man will eat a piece of him!" bellowed Haraldson, kicking up a storm of sparks from the logs in the hearth.

His knuckles glowed bone-white on the shaft of *Heart-Halver*, as if he would throttle the wood.

The smiles froze and fractured and fell from the men's faces.

"No-one was going to," Pieter Magnussen spoke quietly, "We found food."

"We found some stores!" explained Torstein with a little hop, "Some salted fish, some smoked eels, dried meat, beans…"

The skinny Icelander wittered on for quite some time, delighted in his list of provisions. The crew could tell that the jarl was not really listening: Haraldson was nudging the logs back into the fire, the great axe hanging limp by his side.

"… and mead!" finished Torstein triumphantly.

He'd been expecting a cheer: the Vikings could only nod.

The Bjørnson brothers were huddled intently, watching the door and growling behind their hands. With a wave to the captain, Sven motioned that he and the other berserkers would head outside again. Haraldson shook his head vehemently.

A moment passed in which he could plainly see the wolf-men considering whether to disobey him. He was not strong enough against all three of them, and he had already lost face with the earlier mistake. Once, his grip on his crew had been a vice of iron: now, it was… it was a strand of seaweed.

Of all people, it was Torstein who tamed them without even knowing it.

"Dried mushrooms, too: those red ones you find in faerie-rings."

The ones berserkers used for their brew. Haraldson watched the wolf-men stiffen and turn back from the door, their greedy eyes fixed on Torstein. He opened his mouth to speak but Bjørnson was quicker.

"Well then, we're all safe. We'll brew up and show you the magic of the moon!"

Torstein's face went white. "What's it like?"

"Like you've murdered your own guts!" grumbled Pieter Magnussen.

The wolf-man turned slowly and glowered at Magnussen until the long white moustache shivered. "Let's just say, it's not for the old…"

"What else is in the recipe?" asked Torstein.

Now, Sven Bjørnson turned and looked directly at Haraldson.

"We have everything we need."

The old sea-captain felt his insides curdling.

Art by Annabelle Cross

24

Chapter Two

The bones had spoken. Gunnhild Lashtongue packed away her little runes and looked up. The leaden clouds had dropped from the sky and left the stars sharp like shattered glass.

While she watched, a curtain of venomous green light grew and rippled over the slopes of the fjord, towering as high as a fleet of sails.

"You should see this!" she breathed to Januld.

Evidently, he wasn't in the mood for talking.

***

Before Haraldson could stop it happening, Torstein had been escorted to the stores by the pack of wolf-men. The jarl could hear ravens roosting in the roof.

In a storm long ago, when he had been just a boy, the tiller of his knorr had come adrift and floated off over the tide, stolen by the waves. He had that same feeling again now; powerlessly squirming against a force that was dragging him onto the rocks.

He'd seen too much of what the brew gave to a man…

… and what it took.

Pieter Magnussen left with a small gang and returned presently with the headless body. They were muttering together and almost as pale as the corpse itself. Dumping it on a long table at the side of the hall – one of the few yet spared from the fire – they drew close to the hearth, and again cursed the pine needles prickling their feet inside their boots.

The long-hall filled with their reeking stench and Haraldson fought down a retch, tugging his woollen jerkin up over his nose. Someone had found some fairly clean snow and melted it for water in a small pot. As always though, the potful of snow yielded only a pitiful dribble of gritty water: barely enough to dampen their salt-blistered lips.

"Where is Torstein with that mead?" complained Magnussen.

"Mead will muddle your mind," warned Haraldson, "Make you slow and stupid."

"More stupid than Magnussen?" chuckled Ivar Olavson, one of the Danes, "Surely that's not possible?"

"*You* drink it then if you want! It's your funeral!"

Again, he regretted his quick temper. Olavson had meant only to lighten the mood. Magnussen would have found a way to put him in his place with more dignity. The captain was going to speak again, but the Dane avoided his eyes and brooded sullenly into the flames. After a while, he heard the younger man muttering that if *was* to be his funeral, he'd rather depart drunk than sober.

There was a time when *Heart-Halver* would have spoken for the jarl, to silence even the quietest dissent and so be an example to the rest. Tonight though, he pretended not to hear. While the crew thought him dozing again by the fire, he watched them through slit eyelids, and listened to them turning slowly to mutiny… and worse.

***

Gunnhild Lashtongue strapped the quivers of bewitched arrows along each leg and slung the bow tight around her. In the dark of the barrow-mound, she reached down and patted Januld's broken head.

"Cheer up," she whispered, "I'm going to find you some company."

***

The men's voices murmured around the struggling flames: the fear was burning brightly, even if the fire would not.

"So do you think it was the Draugr that wrecked the ship?"

"Ja, of course! To trap us here!"

"No, no, it was the Linnorm – we all saw it!"

"Maybe she bewitched it!"

"Ach! The prow was weak and fell off. We must have hit a skerry."

"We *saw* it, Magnussen!"

"Then you were *drunk*, you half-wit!"

There was a long spell of senseless quarrelling, like dogs barking at each other over a fence. When Haraldson next heard voices, they were hushed. He sensed they were checking if he were awake… so he snored quietly and they went on.

"The jarl is cursed!"

"Ja, it's that wife of his from Grunstrom."

There were some chuckles but the whispering voice became insistent.

"I'm not joking. He took a bride from Grunstrom – she was a *völva*!"

"She was what?"

"Völva – a witch. She knew *galdr* – spell songs… and she could perform *seidr*."

"Ach! You speak too fast! She could do what?"

"She could go into a trance and see the future."

"Sounds like a good choice of wife!" laughed one.

"Ja… except she saw *his* future."

Now their voices shrank even smaller: Haraldson had to strain to hear.

"What do you mean?"

"No-one knows. She just turned on him, screaming and scratching him."

"Sounds like *my* wife…"

"I like it when your wife scratches me!"

More senseless barking followed.

"So what happened to her?"

"He threw her overboard. Told her he'd rather argue with the sea. Then he just sailed off and left her to drown."

There came a low gasp from the crew.

"And now she is *aptrgangr* – walking again."

No words came for a long time but Haraldson could hear the fear crackling in the air.

"What should we do?"

"How should *I* know? I can't see the future!"

Haraldson stood up.

"We kill it."

The circle of warriors flinched as one.

The jarl could see them shooting each other quick glances – how much had he heard?

Eventually, Konyar had the nerve to speak.

Rising slowly to his feet, the Finn asked: "How? How can we kill it?"

Haraldson could feel the men's eyes on him.

"Why don't you ask Arne Vidarson? He seems to know so much."

He stared long and hard at Vidarson, a red-haired brute who had been doing most of the whispering.

Vidarson trembled with shame, but had the sense to keep his mouth firmly shut.

"Well then, I'll tell you about Draugar… what little I know," grunted the jarl.

Heart-Halver was balanced in his hands again, the huge double-blade swinging and twirling in the firelight. "A Draugr supposedly rises to protect its treasure. Well, we've robbed barrow-mounds from Denmark to Vinland and I've never met one yet."

He let the words sink in.

"They're a story told by old mothers to scare their children. Fat kings go to their graves and take their gold with them and always they think – *who will come in the night and steal my gold?* So they tell the world that if any man should, they will ride back on their dead horses from the underworld and hunt them down."

His voice was rising in the hall now, croaking in imitation of the superstitious fishwives he scorned of old: "Oooo! The Draugr is come, swimming through the rock, grown giant as a troll, riding the cattle to death, drinking our blood and driving us mad!"

He laughed at them with contempt.

"If you believe this, you're all already mad!"

The men shuffled from foot to foot, rubbing their chins and stroking their beards. He tried to judge their mood from their battered faces.

Magnusson, the eldest, met his gaze with his own, nodding. He wasn't the superstitious kind.

The Danes, Ivar and Eidur, were smiling at their foolishness.

Vidarson, who earlier had been so full of words that they'd come pouring out, now had none left. He couldn't even look his jarl in the eye.

Yngve the Slav had a face that was impossible to read – but then he never showed much expression. His cheekbones stuck out through his leathery face and his dark eyes were as empty as a dry well.

Konyar the Finn, however, was pointing at the headless body stretched out stiff on the table behind them.

"That's no story told by old mothers."

"No," agreed the jarl, "That's a dead man. But it's not as if it's the first we've ever seen before, is it?"

30

"Well, if it's no Draugr out there," asked Konyar quietly, "What in Hel is it?"

Pieter Magnussen spat into the fire and limped towards the great doors.

"I'm off to turn the snow yellow!" he told them gruffly, "Any of you old mothers care to join me?"

No-one answered, but Haraldson couldn't help but smile. Magnussen might have been the eldest but, by Odin's great grey beard, he was the toughest.

"But grandfather, it's so cold!" laughed Eidur Olavson, seizing the chance of a quick jape, "How will you find your little tap?"

"Ach! *That* one would have trouble on a warm summer's day!" added Ivar, and the pair of brothers howled together.

"Be careful!" warned Arne Vidarson, trying to sound casual but failing… and there it was again: the little fire of fear, crackling again in the logs. No sooner did they put it out, it sprang up afresh.

Magnussen rolled his eyes. "I'll take my shield!" he muttered.

Puzzled, he looked around the walls of the hall.

"Hey! Which of you children has moved my shield?"

They all looked at each other.

Ivar said sadly, "Oh! Now he's so old, he forgets his shield!"

"I bet he's forgotten us already!" Eidur said, equally sadly.

"I've not forgotten wiping snot from your noses – and worse things from worse places when you two were less than my knee!" glowered Magnussen, flapping a raven off his shoulder. "Where is my shield?"

However, the rest were now laughing at him too much to care, so he cursed the lot of them and went without it. It would turn up.

Outside the hall, the fjord was eerily green. Magnussen looked up and caught his breath. He'd seen the aurora before but it always left him feeling like a little boy seeing it for the first time. Moreover, he'd never seen it like this.

Huge sails of vaporous light flapped slowly through the sky, a ghostly luminescence that seemed to ring the horizon like the palisade around the long-hall. Magnussen drifted away, mesmerised by the eldritch glow.

***

Gunnhild Lashtongue was high above, balanced exactly on the upturned keel-bone of the ship once called *Torwurm*, poised like a skua diving for fish. The heavy snow had shrouded the roof: now it glowed softly green with the pulsating witch-light above.

She watched the old one limping out from under the eaves of the roof; heard his slow, crunching footsteps as he wandered beneath her; smelt the rank, damp odour that wafted upwards. Then she struck.

She swung the great shield under her wide-braced feet, crouching low with her arms spread like wings. Skidding faster and faster down the snowy roof, she struck Magnussen just as he was turning.

The edge of the shield bit the old Swede below the ribs, driving him into the frozen ground. Winded like a herring washed up on a sandbank, he floundered and heaved for breath, his eyes and mouth covered with snow.

Behind him, the little völva was getting to her feet. The collision had thrown her rolling in the snow and she'd caught her head against a rock, but the helmet had proven itself.

Magnussen could only watch with bulging eyes as the beak of the owl-shaped visor came closer and closer to his face…

…and the shark-tooth knife drew closer and closer to his throat.

**

On her way back to the round-barrow, Gunnhild passed through the dolmen of rune-stones which leaned in the pine grove, groaning under each other's weight.

She didn't pause to read them: she knew what they said.

Into the surface of each were carved grave-binding inscriptions, none of which had worked.

She skipped into the barrow mound, swinging Magnussen's head by his hair. On her other arm, she carried the shield with the raven emblem.

"Januld will be so pleased," she was saying, "He's been so grumpy but I think he's just lonely."

She held his head up, looking deep into his eyes to

show she was serious, in spite of the skipping. "He hasn't found it easy so he won't talk to me. But *you* – you always know the right thing to say, don't you? You'll put him right in no time."

She skipped onwards, into the dark.

"Hey Januld!" she called, "Look who's come to cheer you up!"

***

In the morning (was it morning? – no real light by which to tell) Haraldson came rolling back off the sea to find the ravens pecking him again. Swatting them away, he felt a bitter irritation that brought him close to tears.

What if he woke one day to find he was too old to drive them off?

Some of the men swore they had heard thunder in the night. The dawn made barely any mark on the skyline. When they went to gather wood, they found Magnussen…

… at least, most of him.

They hauled his headless body onto the table beside Januld's and stood, all of them lost for words and colder than they'd ever felt.

The brightest fire could not settle these shivers.

When the Úlfhédnar heard the news, they swarmed back up into the hall and began sniffing over the ground. Haraldson was dismayed to see that their eyes had already begun to turn, and their teeth chattered from more than just the cold. They were beginning the

Berserkergang: fits and spasms and raging hot flushes that came from the poisons in the mushrooms. Soon, they would *hammask*…

Haraldson didn't want to think about it.

Bjørnson was keenly studying Magnussen's corpse but not, thought the jarl, with any intention of eating it. The wolf-man lifted away the folds of the dead man's clothing to reveal his filthy, dirt-encrusted skin.

Nobody wanted to look… but nobody looked away.

In the cold and from loss of blood, the old man had turned *hel-blár* – deathly blue – but still they could all plainly see the gigantic bruise that slid over Magnussen's belly like a giant purple slug.

"How could a girl strike a blow so hard?" wondered Bjørnson; apparently to himself, for he no longer bothered to even glance at Haraldson.

Ordinarily, one of the Olavson boys would have responded with some witty remark about their Aunt Ingrid… but now, they nodded glumly and remained silent.

It dawned on Haraldson that Magnussen – grouchy, grumbling Magnussen – had always been the one who knew best how to keep their spirits up.

The old goat had left a gaping hole in their family of brothers.

"It *has* to be a Draugr!" protested Vidarson, "It's too strong to be just some feral girl tramping around the woods! Look at that bruise!"

No-one was looking at anything else.

Vidarson was ranting on. "A Draugr has *trollskap* –

shape-shifting magic – and it can grow to the size of a giant! Look, it seized him in its jaws…"

"No, he was killed with his shield," Bjørnson declared flatly.

Vidarson could only goggle at him. "You can't be serious!"

The wolf-man rolled the body over to show the back.

"The bruise is only on the front. There's no puncture in the skin. Nothing seized him in any jaws. The bruise is the shape of a shield edge, driven into him with tremendous force."

Vidarson turned in triumph to the others. "Tremendous force! There! You see?"

The old Bjørnson would have sighed patiently and given Vidarson a weary look. By now though, the wolf-man was too far into *berserkergang*. A rush of rage swept over him. Grabbing Vidarson roughly by the back of the neck, he shoved his face down next to the hideous bruise.

"No! Do *you* see?" he snarled.

Vidarson nodded vigorously several times, desperate to avoid the icy touch of the corpse.

Abruptly, Bjørnson pushed him away and consulted with his wolf-brothers in hushed tones. Ulfgang and Rolf slunk off, sniffing at the doorway for Magnussen's scent…and for any other strange ones.

Torstein saw it was an excellent time to offer around what little food they had since no-one was the slightest bit hungry. Then he sat by the fire, nibbling on a stringy piece of dried meat and gazing into the flames. Haraldson could see the little Icelander was shivering, but somehow doubted that he would have tried the mushrooms.

Konyar the Finn was talking: something in his words tugged at Haraldson's ear, like a hook in a mackerel.

"If Magnussen's body has been outside all night – all morning, whatever it is now – why didn't these damned ravens feed on *him*? Or on Januld, for that matter?"

Arne Vidarson lost no time in seizing on this.

"Have you noticed also that it's always two? Two for each of us. It's not natural."

"So what?" barked Haraldson, "So now your Draugr sends birds to peck us to death?"

Vidarson shot a careful look around to check if Bjørnson had gone – apparently he had. "Maybe not to peck us to death... but to keep us from sleeping. To torment us."

"Ach!" spat Haraldson. He couldn't think what to follow it with.

Outside the hall, the sun barely showed over the ice; simply a smear of orange against the blackness, like a dying coal. How long could they last like this? How long before their dwindling supplies were gone?

How long before they started talking again of eating the dead?

Behind his aching eyelids, he saw the Linnorm again; scales flashing in the storm, writhing across the ribs of the ship, the lizard-lips drawn back over dagger fangs, slithering closer as he fought to hold the tiller.

How long before some nameless horror scuttled back into their pitiful shelter and claimed another head?

Art by Makenzie Stammers

Chapter Three

The wind began to dance with the snow again, whirling the whiteness and whistling under the doors.

Sometime later – impossible to tell how long – Rolf Bjørnson returned, seemingly furred in frost, shivering uncontrollably and pacing the floor. Every now and then, he would pause to bite his leather arm-brace, either to silence his chattering teeth or to endure some hideous agony.

When he tried to speak, he was stammering so badly that it was a long while before anyone could understand him. Sven had to translate while Rolf whimpered and panted and scratched, squatting on his haunches by the feeble fire.

Ulfgang and Rolf had found tracks in the snow, and a trail of blood; little spots of crimson across the ghoulish green-grey drifts. There was a strange scent, too.

They had followed the trail through the woods, and found it led to a *howe* – a barrow-mound or burial tomb – made of evil-looking stones, set into clods of earth in a little pine-grove within the black heart of the forest.

"It *is* a Draugr!" gasped the Danes, "You were right, Vidarson!"

Haraldson swiped at his own eyes. They were blurring again – he needed more sleep maybe. He was trying to persuade men he could barely see anymore.

"Hold your water, boys!" he growled, "Vidarson said that a Draugr will only rise to protect its gold…"

"Ja!" Vidarson glanced warily at the tall wolf-man, but had the courage to speak up, now that everyone was listening. "Its gold, its treasures…"

Now Konyar the Finn cut in: "It took Magnussen's shield…"

"And we never found Januld's helmet!" added Eidur Olavson.

But Haraldson was shaking his head.

"That makes no sense. We haven't offended any spirit! We haven't stolen anything from it! It's stealing from *us*!"

Sven Bjørnson spoke sharply.

"So, you *do* think it's a Draugr?"

The old jarl froze, his blistered lips flapping wordlessly.

The men were all watching him.

Anything he might say next would only come too late – his hesitation had said far too much already.

"It's just some girl…" his voice trailed off.

He wasn't even sure he believed it himself.

By the fire, Rolf said something unintelligible, partly in yelps and barks. He had seized his shield and was gnawing on the edge of it.

"What did he say?"

Sven Bjørnson looked puzzled. "He said she's talking to them in the *howe*."

"Talking to who?"

The wolf-man questioned his brother again but only seemed more puzzled by the answer: "Januld and Magnussen."

Vidarson let out a trembling cry. "That's why it's taking their heads! It's raising them against us! Making them *aptrgangr* – walking again!"

Haraldson scoffed. "They'll have a job walking anywhere without any feet."

"Ja, it's not like Januld was ever that quick on his feet anyway!" quipped Ivar Olavson.

"Maybe he'll be faster without them!" added Eidur.

But Vidarson was insistent and Haraldson saw the men were going to listen to him now. The fear was going to consume them all, however hard they tried to laugh in its face.

"A Draugr cannot be harmed by any weapon forged of iron! It can heal any wound... even grow back dismembered limbs!"

A look of horror fell across Vidarson's haggard face, and he turned to look at the bodies on the table behind them. "We have to move them outside."

Bjørnson shook his head. "No. We may need them."

"What in Hel for?" demanded Konyar.

But the wolf-man had turned to his shivering brother, stroking his straggly hair and tickling him behind the ears. Rolf licked Sven's hands.

"Where is Ulfgang, hey?" Sven asked, in a playful voice.

Again, Rolf yipped and yapped in strange noises the men could not make any sense of – yet his older brother plainly understood. He strode to the doors with Rolf scampering around his legs.

"What is it now?" asked Haraldson, unslinging his axe and following the wolf-men into the night. Without turning to his jarl, Bjørnson began jogging across the crunching, crackling ground.

"He says Ulfgang was going to hunt it on his own."

***

Ulfgang had the scent strongly in his nostrils now. His *berserkergang* surged like lava in his veins. The Draugr was close.

In the gloom, he could make out a break in the line of trees, where a whole rank of them had been flattened by the wind and weight of ice. Their frosty tips hung over a narrow gulley between the cliffs of the fjord.

Down in the water-carved rock, by the flames of a small fire, something was moving.

He had still not fully *hammasked* but he felt strength enough from the raging poisons to kill this Draugr. Rolf might have run off to fetch their brother: Ulfgang meant to show everyone that he was made of sterner stuff. There was a wolf within him now, bursting beneath his skin, tingling in his teeth.

Creeping over the fallen branches, he made his way

along the toppled trunk, out across the gulley, directly over the little witch singing softly below.

Gunnhild Lashtongue was singing a *galdr* over the rune-bones, casting them up and watching how they landed on the ragged cloth she'd spread before the fire. She was puzzled: the little bones kept showing that she would be going on a long journey… but that she could take a short cut.

Something warm and wet landed on her cheek: a dribble of drool. Hot, rancid breath puffed down upon her hair.

She looked up, straight into the wolfish face of Ulfgang Bjørnson.

"Hello, pretty!" he leered.

"Goodbye, ugly!" she smiled.

With a quick slash of the knife, she cut through a short length of rope beside her.

The tall, springy pine tree to which Ulfgang clung had never been blown down by any wind: it had been bent low over the gulley. Suddenly released, it reared like a fresh stallion, shaking free of the snow and bucking Ulfgang high and far across the fjord while his scream faded into the night.

She tilted her head at the rune-bones again and grinned. Now she understood.

It *was* a long journey to the other side of the fjord… but she *did* know a short-cut.

***

Sven Bjørnson held up his hand for quiet and they paused on the frozen snow, their breath like a fog around them.

At first, Haraldson heard nothing.

Then, over their heads, some hellish bird flew, screaming across the sky. Somewhere over on the far side of the fjord, it crashed into the cliffs and fell silent.

"What the devil was that?" hissed the wolf-man.

"It sounded like your brother," Haraldson said grimly.

Exchanging looks, they changed course, wading through the ever-deepening snow towards the crash site.

***

By cutting across the harder ice in the throat of the fjord, skipping and hopscotching across the house-sized chunks of broken glacier, Gunnhild Lashtongue beat the men to it by a good few minutes.

Ulfgang lay like a broken doll on the harsh slopes of rock. Like Magnussen before him, he could only watch the owl-eyed helmet advance upon him, while his tongue hung slackly down his chin.

"Hello again, ugly!" she whispered as she knelt beside him.

The knife sliced easily.

Back at the barrow-mound, she hid Ulfgang's head behind her back.

"Guess what I got you?" she teased the others, before producing it with a flourish. Neither Januld nor Pieter Magnussen showed much interest.

She was hurt.

"Ach! You two are no fun. I thought you'd *like* a puppy…"

***

The Norsemen stood around the three decapitated bodies, like a stone circle. The only sounds were that of Rolf, champing on his shield-edge, and the wind's wickedness outside the door. Konyar could barely croak his words: "What happened to him?"

Haraldson set his jaw and grunted. He would leave it to Bjørnson to tell what little they could. Beside him, the wolf-man brooded under his fanged hood, clenching and unclenching his fists around his claw-knives.

Rolf began to whine, sniffing and licking his dead brother's blood-soaked hands, just as he'd done on the way back from the cliffs. He kept searching at the ragged edges of the neck, as though expecting the head to somehow reappear.

"What happened to him?" asked the Finn again, louder.

Bjørnson's voice was too quiet to hear: they urged him to speak up.

"*It threw him over the fjord!*"

He didn't shout but seemed to howl each word, hurling them up from a husky throat.

The wolf-man glared savagely round at them.

His eyes settled on the jarl.

"We're going to war."

Cautiously, Haraldson folded his arms.

"No, Sven Bjørnson. We have lost too many to lose more. We will stay here, barricade the hall, wait for the spring. When the good light returns, we can repair the ship and get out of here."

"What ship?" demanded Bjørnson bitterly, "There is nothing left! It's just driftwood on the other side of the island!"

But Haraldson was pointing upwards, at the roof of the great long-hall.

"*Torwurm.*"

The Vikings gazed around in wonder and dawning realisation… then started to chatter excitedly. It could be done! There was hope after all -

The wolf-man's harsh snarl cut off the noise.

"NO!"

All eyes turned upon him. He stalked the hall, twitching with the poison in his veins, frothing from the mouth. The whites of his eyes were red-raw, the swollen pupils like two black moons. When he spoke next, his own stuttering enraged him, so that he forced each word out in a guttural bark:

"N-NOT W-WAIT-ING F-FOR SH-SH-SH-SHIP!"

His lips drew back and he panted, his tongue lolling out. The spasm of rage seemed to pass, at least for the moment.

He began again, fighting to control his own voice.

"We're not waiting for the spring. We're going to make a stronger brew and we'll all drink. We're going to feast on this Draugr."

He shot a look at Torstein, who squirmed quickly backwards. Then the Úlfhédnar fixed his fevered stare back on Haraldson.

The jarl could see what was coming: he didn't need any rune-bones.

"What say *you*, Leif Haraldson?" It was a challenge, blunt and deadly.

Haraldson shifted his feet ready, slowly unfolding his arms but keeping them loose at his side. He made no move for his axe.

Calmly, he repeated: "I say we wait for spring and sail this ship home."

The wolf-man opened his mouth – and *now* Haraldson pounced, not with blades but words; words which pounded like fists. His voice roared to its topmost crest and crashed against their eardrums.

"I say you're a fool, robbed of his wits by toadstools! You'd poison the rest of us, and have us all scratching around in the dark, like dogs! Look at your brother!"

The jarl stabbed a frost-bitten finger towards Rolf: "Shaking like a leaf and chewing his shield! Dribbling all over the floor!"

The crew were all watching. He had them now. He used to think he was losing them… but he had them back now. He should have known when to stop.

"Look at your other brother!"

He pointed to Ulfgang – or at least, the bits they'd managed to scrape off the cliff – and immediately sensed his mistake.

The fire flickered in the hearth and Bjørnson's rage

was coming to the boil again. Desperately, Haraldson tried to make his point... but he knew it would be worthless now.

"You want to end up like this?"

"You're scared!" sneered the wolf-man, "You're scared of it."

The wise old jarl took a deep breath; then, spoke quietly. "Ja, I'm scared. Only an idiot with fungus in his head would say he were not."

He glanced around at the crew's faces. Magnussen would have seen the sense of what he said – probably even added another serene pearl of wisdom – but Magnussen was gone.

The few men left were showing shock and even revulsion on their faces. They had just heard their jarl admit that he was frightened. What good was a frightened jarl?

"You know who she is, don't you?" asked Bjørnson, drawing closer.

Haraldson knew now in his heart: he was finished.

"What else do you know?" snarled the berserker.

"Nothing!"

The frozen air between them hissed with their breath.

The wolf-man sprang at him, clawing through his furs into his flesh – and not one of the old jarl's men stepped in to help him. With empty eyes, they watched as Bjørnson ripped at his sides, and tore the old wound in his shoulder until the arm hung useless.

Like a spider in the shadows, Gunnhild Lashtongue was watching too.

***

Outside the hall, the night murdered the daylight almost the instant it was born. The waves of sea-slush slopped on the shore and the sorrowful moan of a whale echoed across the fjord from far out across the heaving ice-floes. The moon prowled over the horizon, blood-red like Odin's eye.

Eirik Blacktooth's mighty long-hall was filling with evil fumes: Rolf and Sven Bjørnson, the Úlfhédnar, were brewing up in the cauldron over the fire.

They had used most of the mead to bolster the effects… together with grubby handfuls of other mysterious ingredients which they refused to name.

Torstein watched nervously the whole time, trying to make out what the wolf-brothers said to each other.

"This time," he heard Sven mutter, "don't add the elf-caps 'til the end."

Rolf seemed to quietly whine a question.

"All of it," replied Sven, "And the meat."

Torstein was puzzled. He thought all the meat was finished yesterday… or last night… or whatever men called it up here in the ever-dark.

"Hey Rolfie!" called Konyar the Finn, "Tell me again – what does it feel like, this *Berserkergang*?"

Rolf simply panted, blinking in the firelight and licking his lips… but Sven looked across at them: Torstein with his anxious eyes; Konyar and Yngve, holding cloaks over their noses; Vidarson, tugging at his red beard; and the Olavson brothers sharpening their spears.

The wolf-man twisted his lip. "Not pleasant at first – like you see here with Rolf: twitches, shivers, stammering. But that's only the beginning."

As he twirled the ladle in the pot, something gristly turned over in the broth.

"This is our father's recipe," continued the wolf-man, dreamily, "He came from the great lake at Vättern and sailed with Valdemar the Dreadful, all the way to the western lands beyond Vinland."

The brew sploshed and bubbled.

"He learned *trollskap* from the Skraelings there: a killing magic. Magic to bring out the wolf in each of us."

He poured some of the brew into a horn-cup and sprinkled some of the dried mushrooms over the top. Looking up at the others, he bared his long, white teeth.

"With this, you will *hammask* – shed your human skin and release the true beast hidden within. You will feel some pain but it becomes good pain."

Now, Torstein was truly mystified. "A *good* pain?"

"Ja! Ja!" insisted the Berserker, "Pain begins to feel good. You will run free under the moon, stronger than you have ever felt; able to kill a man with a single blow. You will feel no wound, not even if a spear went through you."

He seized a blazing branch from the fire… and bit it off in his mouth.

The Norsemen leapt up but, as the wolf-man

continued to chew the burning wood, perfectly calmly, they relaxed and even laughed in amazement.

"That's going to truly hurt in the morning!" Torstein winced.

Bjørnson swallowed and grinned with sooty teeth.

"Up here, the morning never comes!"

The brew was ladled out to each of them and they stood, hesitating, waiting for someone else to drink first. Finally Yngve, the silent Slav, lost his patience and emptied his cup in a single gulp. Wiping his bristled mouth, he burped loudly and shrugged at the others.

Konyar the Finn laughed aloud and drained his cup too. The Olavsons clinked their cups in a toast to each other's health and, cautiously, Vidarson tipped back his own cup.

The mead instantly brought a warm glow to their cheeks, as if lava were sliding into their belly. There were straggly bits left between their teeth to chew through but –

"That's really not bad!" laughed Ivar Olavson.

"I was expecting much worse!" agreed Eidur.

Torstein was still holding his cup.

"Drink, little Torstein!" they taunted.

"I've been thinking…" he began, "One of us ought to stay sober… just in case."

"In case of what?" the others roared, outraged that he was not joining them. How typical of the cowering, rat-faced man!

"Well… in case it goes wrong."

They laughed at him. "What could go wrong?"

Torstein looked anxiously over to where the old jarl lay, slumped with his back against a post. "Someone should watch him."

"Ach! The old goat is dead – or dying. There's nothing to be done for him now."

The crew pressed in on all sides around him... but Torstein shook his head and stubbornly refused to drink.

Exasperated but merry with the mead, the others turned their backs on him in contempt and headed out over the snow, jogging with their weapons swinging, towards the Draugr's barrow-mound.

The little Icelander heard their boisterous singing vanish into the night and turned back towards his jarl. Kneeling beside the broken man, he shook his shoulder.

"Lief Haraldson? Can you hear me?"

He listened for a breath: there was none. He splashed water in the man's face, he banged the pot with the ladle, he shouted, he prayed, he wept.

After a while, he despaired; sure that the jarl was dead.

Hidden above him in Torwurm's ribs, Gunnhild slipped silently out.

Chapter Four

The scarlet moon had turned the snow to frozen blood, spattered over the fjord, dripping from the lines of pine-spears and clotting on the crew's steaming backs.

Bjørnson and his brother had stripped to the waist, their filthy wolf-skins blowing tatty and grey in the icy wind.

"You are Úlfhédnar now!" he roared over the thunder in their eardrums.

Their running feet picked up pace as the power pounded through their veins; their laughter and battle-songs turned to howls and barks; they fell to all fours and flew across the snow. Reaching the treeline and the trail that led to the Draugr's barrow-mound, they scattered into the wild woods, frenzied with the thirst for blood.

The Olavsons found themselves together in a snow-packed clearing, feeling like two shrieking boys again. They pelted each other with snowballs, then rolled up a giant ball and placed a smaller one upon it, for a head. Ivar plastered the snowman's chin with more handfuls of snow, sculpting a beard, and Eidur howled with glee as he recognised their old lately-departed sea-captain.

Standing together, they hefted their mighty spears. Eidur held aloft his *höggspjót* with its blade grinning wide in the moonlight, while Ivar twirled his *krókspjót* with its cruel barbs facing backwards from the tip, like a monstrous silver pinecone.

Ivar threw first – and missed hopelessly. As so often happened, the little hooks on the shaft of the spear caught on his throwing arm, and the *krókspjót* plunged harmlessly to the side of Haraldson the Snowman.

Eidur howled again with hysterical laughter.

"See, little brother: this is how a man throws!" he teased, and sent his *höggspjót* carving through the snowman's head.

Ivar scowled. "The hooks get tangled. It was made by an idiot."

"Who is the greater idiot: the one who made it or the one who stole it?"

Ivar felt a great wave of rage surging up from his knees, and charged his brother – but Eidur was gone, rolling and tumbling down the drifts of snow, cackling at the moon.

Snatching up his useless spear, Ivar battled to catch up. He found his infuriating brother doubled up against the trunk of a tree, heaving hoarsely for breath.

"So, you can throw but you can't run!"

But Eidur was struggling with something trapped around his throat. Something heavy dropped through the frozen branches, snapping and crashing.

Ivar watched his brother jerk upwards, hoisted into the air. Amidst horrible choking noises and frantically kicking feet, the Dane saw that his brother's neck was tangled in a noose, counter-balanced by a gigantic log.

He leapt up into the branches and hacked at the rope with his knife and the pair of brothers fell, breathless, onto a pile of sticks and fallen branches…

…into the pit of sharpened stakes below.

***

Gunnhild Lashtongue skipped back to the barrow-mound, swinging a head in each hand like a milk-maid with her churns. She put them carefully with the others, expecting that at least Magnussen would welcome the Danes to the *howe*… but it seemed they were all sulking at her now.

Sighing, she turned to inspect the spears and immediately, her mood brightened.

Her treasure trove was growing nicely.

***

Haraldson was stumbling through a blizzard of white pain, every step an agony of exhaustion. The wind screamed and tore at his wounds with corpse-cold claws. His tortured eyeballs shivered in their sockets like bats in a cave.

The Linnorm slid towards him…

He jerked awake to find the ravens pecking again,

perched on his chest and plucking at his tired carcass. With blood-chilling horror, he realised he was too weak to fight them off any more. He was waking from one nightmare into another.

He sobbed with despair while their merciless beaks stabbed him again and again; their tiny black eyes, devoid of compassion or remorse.

"Let me die!" he begged his gods.

Then he cursed them and cried out for help.

Looking round, he could only see the headless bodies of his crew, piled up on the table on the other side of the hall. The rest were gone. There was no help.

The ravens kept feeding.

And then help came… in the shape of Torstein.

Shooshing the birds away, he gripped the jarl's good shoulder and gawped, delighted and relieved, at Haraldson's ruined face.

"I knew you wouldn't die!" Torstein was laughing, with tears down his cheeks, "I *knew* you wouldn't die!"

"I might have to one day," grunted Haraldson.

"Here," urged Torstein, holding a horn-cup to the old jarl's lips, "Drink this."

Haraldson nearly did. Then his old nose caught a whiff of something evil and he roughly cast the drink away. "NO!"

"You need to get your strength back," argued the rat-faced man, "before they come back."

"I'm not drinking *that*." Haraldson's voice was flat and final.

Torstein sagged backwards. "Then… they're going to

kill us," the little Icelander whined, hugging his knees, "and then they're going to eat us."

"Ach!" growled Haraldson, "If the ravens leave anything…"

Torstein nodded glumly. "Odin has two ravens – Huginn and Muninn."

"Any good sea-captain would: they'll find you land."

But Torstein wasn't listening… he was looking into the flames. "Huginn is thought, Muninn is memory. What if this Draugr has enchanted these birds to take our thoughts, our memories?"

Haraldson looked at him sharply. "These birds were brought here by earlier explorers; probably Eirik Blacktooth himself, you rabbit-brained idiot."

But Torstein glowered back over the fire. "Still you won't see it, will you?"

Haraldson rubbed his eyes; half as a joke, half because they were blurry again.

"Won't see what?"

Torstein's finger pointed through the flames at him. "You're cursed."

"Ach!" spat Haraldson.

"You're haunted by that girl."

Haraldson tried to laugh but found his ribs couldn't bear to.

"You know her don't you?" Torstein insisted, rising to his feet like an Icelandic geyser, "She's your wife, isn't she? Or she was – before you threw her off the ship!"

The old jarl's mouth stayed shut, but the teeth could be heard gritting and grinding behind his beard.

"She was a völva, wasn't she? She bewitched the ship, made the *Linnorm* turn on us, left us shipwrecked here… and now she's killing us one by one! I'm right, aren't I?"

But the jarl's eyes burned back at him in an iron silence.

Torstein sagged again, like a torn sail.

"It doesn't matter anyway now. The others all turned into Úlfhédnar. They're going to tear out our throats!" he sobbed, "We're all going to die up here in the dark."

"As long as they tear out your throat first so I don't have to hear you bleating!" muttered Haraldson.

Torstein sniffed and looked at him bitterly. "You know what their secret ingredient was? How they passed the magic on to each other? Why Rolf and Ulfgang went wild first?"

Wiping his nose, he leaned forward. His ratty face was red from the fire.

"Sven ate the elf-caps first. Then he passed the magic to the other two *in his water*."

Torstein let the last words dig in deep enough.

Haraldson's nose wrinkled.

"It's worse," Torstein went on.

For a moment Haraldson was lost, wondering what *worse* could be, but then his tired ears caught up with Torstein's galloping mouth… and he heard the worst.

While the others had debated using their dead shipmates for food or as bait for traps, Bjørnson had whispered to Rolf: "We need the hearts for the brew."

After a long time, Torstein hoped aloud:

"Maybe he won't come back."

But the wolf-man did come back, much later, slinking through the high doors while Haraldson shivered next to a dead fire.

***

Yngve and Konyar were trying to hunt silently in the snow but, behind them, Arne Vidarson was prattling on about Draugar lore.

It wasn't helping the hunt and it wasn't helping their nerve.

They had come across the dolmen of rune-stones and Vidarson had deciphered the inscriptions. Now, he was jabbering in a hoarse whisper and each of the others felt his own heart rattling his rib-cage.

The brew had taken them deep into *berserkergang*: their eyes had widened in the gloom and the ghostly outlines of the frosted forest left blurred traces skidding across their vision. Their breath poured from their hot throats like volcanic steam; they twitched and squirmed in every muscle, jaws clamped and backs arching, picking their way up a steep trail beside a frozen gorge.

A little way up the trail, hidden beneath a shroud of snow, Gunnhild Lashtongue lay on her back with the *krókspjót*.

Ivar Olavson had never known the purpose of the little hooks set into the shaft, only that they spoiled his aim… but the völva knew.

Bunching her knee up to her chest, she wriggled her

bony toes behind the hooks and rested the razor-sharp spear-head on a cleft stick, pushed into the ground.

"This is how a girl throws!" she hissed.

As the last of the men came around the trees, falling into line with the others, she snapped her foot forward, flinging the spear with animal ferocity.

At the front, Konyar the Finn felt as if he'd been punched in the chest by a bear. He looked down to find a good two feet of spear-shaft left protruding through his broken chain-mail. Behind him, Yngve found himself skewered on the remaining eight feet: the pinecone-shaped head was embedded in his ribs.

Dreamily, Konyar grabbed the spear-shaft and pulled himself off it; as he did so, the vicious barbs twisted his shipmate's splintered ribs and the Slav, normally such a quiet man, shrieked in agony.

Arne Vidarson stepped up behind to support Yngve's shoulders…

… and Gunnhild sprang out of the dark, flying across the rocks. Kicking the foot of the *krókspjót*, she drove the head all the way through Yngve and into Vidarson.

With his mouth frozen open, coughing up blood, Vidarson was knocked from his feet by the sheer force of the blow.

Gunnhild seized the shaft of the spear left sticking out of Yngve and heaved to the left, as if hauling on an oar: Vidarson was dragged out over the edge of the gorge. His body-weight now drove Yngve to his knees and Vidarson felt himself dangling, the murderous spear-tip beginning to rip its way out of his chest.

The völva gripped the end of the spear in her blackened claw, but the combined weight of the men was tipping the balance. She glanced over her shoulder at Konyar, who was still probing the gory hole where the *krókspjót* had pierced through.

"I can't hold it!" she told him, urgently.

Instinctively, he dropped his swords and snatched the shaft from her failing grip. She smiled gratefully. Then, with a simple swing of the *höggspjót*, she cut off his head.

For a while, his hands held their position on the spear-handle but eventually, in the absence of any further orders from the brain, they quietly deserted.

Screaming with terror, Yngve finally pitched backwards over the edge, and he and Vidarson plunged into the gorge.

Vidarson had time to marvel that the Slav knew a great many words after all, for he was using every single one on the way down, very rapidly.

Then they bounced raggedly on the ice and were smashed to splinters.

***

Using Magnussen's shield as a toboggan, and Eidur's wide-bladed *höggspjót* as both paddle and rudder, Gunnhild Lashtongue slid her way down the slopes to the base of the frozen falls. She was delighted to find that the *krókspjót* had survived the fall... even if the same could hardly be said for Yngve and Vidarson.

Initially, Vidarson felt as if he had landed in a pile of

wet rope. As the white-furred witch lifted him up however, he realised it had been his own intestines.

Triumphantly, he thought: *So, I was right about the Draugr!*

Then he looked into her soot-striped face, and suddenly wished he wasn't.

***

Gunnhild tied the heads to the spear-shaft, using their greasy plaits to secure them, and sang lullabies to them as she set off across the snow, under the blood-stained moon. Halfway to the barrow, she had a sudden thought and went back for the intestines.

***

Foxfire prickled and played over the mossy stones of the round-barrow and the völva's impatient voice drifted out of the dark, over the snow.

"Settle down, boys!" she scolded them, "First you won't talk: now, I can't shut you up. One at a time, one at a time! Pieter Magnussen, what say you? ... Ja, now you can see all the little clues! ... Of course! But Konyar and Yngve weren't with us when I told you *that* bit... No, Vidarson, you're mistaken. Why don't you let him talk? ... Ach! What is it *now* Ulfgang? No, I've already told you: we can go later... Now, Ivar! Eidur! What would your Aunt Ingrid say if she heard you talk like that? ... Ulfgang! ... Yes, I *know* but you'll see them soon, I promise… Hey! Rat-face! Don't do that…"

Eventually, her little soot-black head emerged from the barrow stones and she sat in the moonlight, casting her bones to see the way ahead. She frowned.

"Why must I clean the shield?" she wondered.

She knew better than to question the bones, so she hurried back inside the barrow and dabbed at Magnussen's shield with the hem of her fur cloak until the answer shone through.

Under the shreds of leather, there were two ravens, not one, emblazoned on the wood.

She was going to need a hunting partner.

Pulling a long, bone whistle from her furs, she pressed it to her shrivelled lips and blew a long, haunting note. It whined in the wind, and wound its way up into the ice-capped mountains.

***

Rolf snivelled and pressed against Bjørnson's legs. Both Úlfhédnar heard the sound, shrill and clear above the blowing snow and the hammering of their hearts.

Sven ruffled his brother's fur, grinning with lupine glee. "She's calling for help!"

Rolf laid his head on his brother's knee and snuffled. Sven thumped his nose.

"It means she's scared, you bone-headed mutt!"

But Rolf had been the one to find the Olavsons' mangled bodies, spiked on stakes in the pit beneath the noose-tree, both headless. Later, the shivering wolf-men

63

had heard Vidarson and Yngve screaming in the dark and crashing down the gorge.

This was a hunt turning against them.

With his brother cursing behind him, Rolf bolted back to the long-hall.

***

The creature called Sköll came creeping down out of the mountains, his monstrous muscles rippling like lake-water under his clotted fur; yellow teeth bared in a cruel, slavering maw.

His lamp-bright eyes blinked slowly, and he pricked his tattered ears towards the singing from the barrow-mound.

He'd met this völva before, serving her whenever she had summoned him. Now he was eager to serve again: she always found him good meat.

Sure enough, there she stood in the shadows of the woods, holding out her dripping hands. He could smell something that flooded his mouth with saliva.

"Look, Sköll!" she was calling, happily, "I got you sausages!"

The huge, hairy beast thanked her with his great, sad eyes…

… and took her offering.

She hummed contentedly, watching him feed, and patted his matted fur. Sköll had never once spoken a word to her, but he was always better company than any of this god-forsaken crew.

"Three more heads," she purred, looking up at the crystal stars, "and then we're done."

**

Haraldson woke from a sweat-soaked sleep, to find Rolf sniffing and licking his face. Cuffing him away, he looked around the hall for any sign of Sven.

If the wolf-man was still alive, he had not yet returned.

The old jarl breathed out.

His next thought was that Torstein must have let the fire go out in the night, and he roared a thousand curses into the echoes of the long-hall.

Torstein was lying on the other side of the hall: Haraldson could see his boots behind the cauldron used for the brew, now upturned on the filthy floor. Evidently, the little rat-faced man was too exhausted or drunk to move, or even wake, for he ignored the loudest and most ferocious threats that Haraldson could muster. In the end, Rolf used his teeth to drag Torstein into the moonlight which slid through the chimney-hole.

The little Icelander was *nár-fölr* – corpse white.

His head was gone.

While Haraldson goggled at the dead man, Sven Bjørnson crept back into the long-hall, seething through clenched teeth.

Even Rolf shrank from him now.

Art by Annabelle Cross

Chapter Five

The Úlfhédnar was beginning to hammask. He barely looked like a man anymore. Sniffing his way around the hall, he was in constant movement, constant agitation, swinging his head from side to side with his long tongue steaming between his hanging jaws. His eyes were wide and wild, blood-shot and scowling and hungry.

When he saw Haraldson trying to struggle upright against the post, his hackles rose and his ruined lips curled, dripping with froth. Slowly, he drew up from all fours and seemed to balance like a great hound on its hind legs, his forepaws dangling in front of him.

The old jarl was struck by an odd thought: was he a man becoming a wolf – or a wolf that had become a man?

To his surprise, he realised the wolf-man was snarling words at him.

"You lost us another shipmate, then?" Bjørnson was nodding towards Torstein.

Haraldson harrumphed. "Just the one. How many did you lose?"

The wolf-man's snarl slashed wider into his savage face and he prowled the floor, his furious eyes smouldering up at the old jarl.

"It's just you and me left. Just like old times."

Haraldson began to chuckle, which did nothing to improve the berserker's mood.

"What's so funny?"

The jarl wiped his eyes.

"Just like old times?" he mocked Bjørnson with a sneer, "Sometimes it seems as if there were no other times. Killing and looting and grave-robbing: exactly what is it you miss about the old times?"

Above them, a raven flapped its wing.

The wolf-man stared back from hollow eye-sockets.

"I miss…" he trailed off.

"What?" hissed Haraldson in the chilly half-light of the long-hall.

"I miss feeling alive," the wolf-man sighed, "That's why we drink the brew: it helps us remember the life we had."

"No," the jarl shook his head, "it makes you forget it."

Bjørnson was nosing through the puddles of brew spilt over the floor, and Haraldson laughed again. "It's all gone. She must have poured it out when she killed Torstein."

But the wolf-man smiled. Pulling a goatskin bag from his waist, he brought it towards Haraldson. "I saved most of it before we left. Here!"

Haraldson felt suddenly dizzy and clung to the post.

"Keep that away from me!" he whispered hoarsely.

Sven snapped his fingers at his cringing brother: Rolf crept forwards, taking another swig from the bag of brew. Instantly, the scrawny little wolf-man seemed to swell in size, bristling with fur and bulging with brawn.

Together, the Úlfhédnar circled Haraldson while he slumped against the post, sick with weariness and ache and fear.

"Keep back!" he roared – but his roar was weak and hollow, and carried no force.

They closed in, Rolf seizing his broken arm and twisting, until the jarl's mouth opened in agonised protest – and Sven slopped the brew down his tortured throat. Spit and splutter as he might, he felt the fiery mixture trickling into his belly. They forced him to swallow most of the bag then drained the remains between them.

Finally, they sat back with glowing eyes, watching and waiting for Leif Haraldson to *hammask*.

***

Haraldson was sliding across the blood-slicked deck, his stomach heaving; his brow white and drenched with sweat. In his ears, the shrieks of his crew stuck like knives. His grip was slipping on the sticky handle of Heart-Halver, and the scarlet light of the moon butchered every surface.

They were pitching and rolling in a sea of gore: spray spattered the sails as if spouting from severed arteries.

The *Linnorm* rode the waves at the prow of the ship,

its reptilian head snaking over the churning red surf, devouring the tide in great, greedy gulps.

Creaking in the timbers of the ship, it corkscrewed its neck, rearing up over the mast and the rows of oars, striking down through its own ribs…

**

Hunched on his haunches out on the snowy slopes of the woods, Haraldson gazed with swollen eyes at the blood-stained moon. He flexed his bad shoulder and found there was no pain, only a gritty, grinding sensation in the socket of his arm. Rolf had held him down while Sven screwed it back in, telling him in soothing tones that the brew would soon take all the pain away: it would make the pain good.

The Úlfhédnar had been right: Haraldson felt good and strong and alive. He felt like a man he had somehow forgotten to be. He wanted to race under the moon and sink his fangs into flesh… which was odd because he had a full belly already. Before leaving the hall, the three of them had feasted well.

The wolf-brothers had scampered off into the night, too impatient for the old jarl's *berserkergang* to catch up with their own. He could hear howls high up on the slopes of the fjord and felt briefly sorry for the little völva.

Then something was coming, crashing through the trees; something dark-furred and deep-growling; something relentless and heartless and mindless.

Haraldson forced himself to breathe slowly; braced his

feet against the rock and stood his ground, his eyes narrowed to arrow-slits against the spitting ice.

The hairy monster roared and pounced – and *Heart-Halver* swung in a flashing arc, biting deep into the beast's flesh.

There was a yowl and the dire creature skidded past him in the snow, showering him with its lifeblood and scratching at his eyes as it tumbled. For a second, it scrabbled frantically for a footing in the drifts... before the old jarl brought his axe down upon its fur-capped skull.

Haraldson stood, panting and exhilarated, exalting in the triumph of the kill.

Lifting his head to the sky, he let out a long, lung-bursting roar of primal fury and sated blood-lust. The echoes ghosted back and forth over the ice.

With the haft of his axe, he turned the carcass over ... and found Rolf's sightless eyes rolling towards his own.

Somewhere in the woods, he heard the soft, mischievous giggling of a young girl.

***

Gunnhild Lashtongue was crouching beneath the pines, checking her bones quickly. Once again, the runes were puzzling her: a giant wolf was coming. Shrugging carelessly, she wrapped them in the dirty scrap of cloth.

Sven Bjørnson landed in the snow not three feet from where she stood, his hackles rising like a ridge of rock along his spine, his canines glistening in his evil smile.

He stepped purposely forward, menacing and sinister.

Gunnhild's bow was still slung over her shoulder; the spears were back at the barrow; her shark-tooth knife was sheathed in her furs.

She held the wolf-man's gaze and did not blink.

The grey-furred Úlfhédnar advanced again, deadly and deliberate.

"Hey, little girl!" his growl was rich and satisfied, "Time to feed the Big Bad Wolf!"

She held a hand to her mouth and giggled.

"You silly man!" she laughed, "You're not the Big Bad Wolf."

She was pointing a black-boned finger behind him: "*He* is."

Bjørnson became aware of a hulking presence behind him in the trees; something that panted hot gouts of foul-smelling fog; something with filthy, shaggy hair and a lethal arsenal of fangs and claws.

Sköll, the great mountain wolf, locked his jaws around Bjørnson's neck.

***

On the way back to the round-barrow, Gunnhild stopped to ask the Úlfhédnar if the pain was still good: Bjørnson refused to comment on the matter so she bashed his head against each passing tree-trunk and repeated her question every time. Maybe he got a little punch-drunk, for he never spoke a word.

Sköll wanted to stay – he sensed more good prey out there in the dark – but Gunnhild hushed him and fed him more sausage. Stroking his mighty head, she reassured him that he had done more than enough already.

"This last one," she murmured, "I can finish myself."

***

Haraldson woke to the caw of the ravens. It seemed to him that every raven on the damned island must have come to feast. They swarmed over his tattered body in a black storm of beating wings and jabbing beaks, until he whirled his axe in a tempest of his own rage, and the dreadful birds retreated to the treetops.

Finding scraps of meat in his teeth, he shuddered and tried to forget the night before... and every night before that.

He found Bjørnson's headless body in the woods and sat down heavily, knowing he was the last. It was just him now... him alone against the wind and the ice and the dark... and the Draugr.

With his aching feet prickling with pine needles, the old jarl set his jaw and made his way back to where Rolf lay. He tugged his furs tightly around himself, and burrowed his head down into his sore and weary shoulders. He laid the mighty *Heart-Halver* across his lap but kept the handle firmly in his ragged hands.

When she came to take Rolf's head, he would be waiting for her.

***

In the round *howe* of hulking stones, Gunnhild Lashtongue addressed the crew; not skipping up and down now, but standing proud and defiant; her clawed hands on her bony hips, her harsh words of chastisement blazing in the dark of the barrow.

"One more stand, my Vikings!" she hissed with eyes as sharp as ravens', "One more stand and it's done. Bring him to me."

In the darkened long-hall of Eirik Blacktooth, the gnawed and headless bodies of Januld the Walrus, Pieter Magnussen and Torstein rose ponderously to their feet and shuffled towards the door.

Behind them, Ulfgang slithered across the floorboards with his broken leg-bones scratching against the wood.

From the pit of stakes deep in the woods, crawled the Olavsons; Konyar slipped and stumbled down the rocky trail that led to the gorge; Yngve and Vidarson crawled, and pulled their shattered bodies over the frozen river.

Leaving deep gouges in the snow, the headless men converged on the old jarl while he waited, shivering in the dark and the cold.

Haraldson heard them coming through the ever-night, saw their outlines against the charcoal sky and felt dread rob him of the power to think. Their helmets squatted on their shoulders, filled only with the blackest emptiness. He laid about him with the axe but knew he could not defeat them all. He had brought them to their deaths once already: he could not bear to slay them again.

With stone-cold hands they plastered his eyes with snow, hoisted him aloft and carried him, howling with terror, through the lines of trees, past the dolmen of binding-stones and into the yawning mouth of the barrow-mound.

***

Haraldson was adrift, a small boy again, floating on his tiller-less knorr on a becalmed sea. There was not even a whisper of a breeze: the water lapped at the side of the boat like a litter of kittens. An endless, flat expanse of seal-grey ocean stretched to the horizon in every direction with not a hint of where dry land might lie. His raven scratched at its cage door.

Something vast and muscular slid under the hull, silent and hidden beneath him.

He jerked awake.

The ice-bright eyes of Gunnhild Lashtongue were burning into his own.

"We meet again, you old rogue!" smiled the little völva.

He felt sick and dizzy and light-headed, unable to feel his hands or feet. The stout stones of the barrow-mound rose on all sides, throbbing with a pulse of their own.

The witch-light of the aurora flickered green and lilac over the island, bathing the trees in a poisonous iridescence. In the centre of the *howe*, a tiny fire spat sparks towards the rocky roof, throwing long shadows across her tiger-striped face.

"What a happy reunion!" she rejoiced, clapping her clawed hands and bobbing her head excitedly.

In the feeble half-light of the barrow, Haraldson could make out flat stone arches over the burial chambers that ringed the mound. In each one, nailed to short wooden posts by their plaited pony-tails and braided beards, there hung the mangled heads of his crew.

A howl of anguish rose in the semi-darkness, and Haraldson dimly realised it had come from him.

He caught his breath and remembered: he was a jarl, a chief, a sea-captain. With these men, he had been the scourge of the Northern coasts, a fearless warrior, a Viking. His last words on this earth were not going to be the pathetic squeals of a runt piglet.

He forced his exhausted eyes to meet hers and began to curse her with the darkest of hexes; he cursed her ancestors to rise against her and avenge him; he cursed every descendant she would ever have to be blind and brain-fevered, disfigured and deformed.

"Vengeance shall be mine, Draugr!" he finished.

Then he sank back and waited for the final horror to be over.

Her eyes were wide with shock and she sat back, trembling. For a while, she struggled to speak, holding her bony hands over her mouth and rocking to and fro.

When she recovered herself and spoke next, the old jarl grew cold: cold with the realisation that her trembling had nothing to do with fear. She was simply amused.

"Draugr?" she giggled incredulously, "You silly old man. *I'm* not the Draugr!"

Haraldson swore at her in exasperation. "Then whose *howe* is this?"

She grew more serious and leaned closer, her soot-blackened lips nearly touching his.

"This is the *howe* of Eirik Blacktooth."

The old jarl breathed slowly out.

So this was what had become of the mighty explorer and his people. This was why his great long-hall was left desolate and cold in the dark.

"What happened to him?" he asked in a tiny voice, hardly daring to know the truth.

The völva's eyes travelled far away as she told the long and bitter story of Eirik Blacktooth, like a skald telling ghost stories around the fire back home.

Torwurm had come out of the fog, years before, bearing Blacktooth and his savage crew of men to this barren, ice-ravaged land. He'd been a voracious killer, merciless in his cruelty, insatiable in his lust for blood. When the pirate finally died, it had not been in the glory of battle – no Valkyrie had ridden down to carry him to Valhalla – he had been murdered by some of his own men, poisoned and beaten and abandoned.

"The remainder of his men laid him in this *howe*, sacrificing his finest warriors so that they might escort him," explained the witch, "but a man left to die sitting up cannot pass into the next world."

Haraldson found he was barely breathing now.

"When the winter came and the sun left this land, he became *aptrgangr* – a Draugr – possessed of dreadful powers…"

"*Trollskap!*" muttered Haraldson: Arne Vidarson had been right after all.

The little völva nodded.

"Ja, *trollskap*. No weapon of iron could harm him or the men he raised from the dead. Any wound they suffered would heal the next winter: their mouldy limbs grew back, even if severed from their body. They raided every settlement, razed every village, took countless lives… and piled their treasures high, here in the mound."

Glimmering in the firelight, Haraldson could make out his crew's prized possessions: the Olavsons' spears, Magnussen's raven-badged shield, Januld's owl-faced helmet, Konyar's fine suit of chain-mail.

"But what does he want with us?" demanded Haraldson, trying to keep the whining note out his voice, "We have never robbed this grave!"

The witch shook her head. "You don't understand. Let me explain."

She drew her knees up to her chest, and hugged her skeletal arms around them, her breath like wisps of mist in the cold of the barrow.

"Not all Draugar rise to reclaim their trinkets. Sometimes a man's deeds in life mark him to be so truly evil, that he rises as *aptrgangr* anyway. Eirik Blacktooth was such a man – if indeed, we can call him a man."

She gazed into the flames. "He was an Úlfhédnar: he already knew the secret of the elf-caps, the strength and power and rage they brought on…"

Haraldson had a dark premonition of her next words.

"But on his travels in the west, he met shamans who showed him how to brew a stronger mixture, even more terrible, using foul ingredients."

"The flesh of the dead!" guessed Haraldson.

The witch nodded sadly.

"Ja: the hearts of humans. With this brew, the wolf-men would pass through their fits of shivers and finally *hammask*: change into something unspeakably evil. Eirik Blacktooth could never die."

Haraldson grew suspicious.

"Yet, in all our time on this damned island, we've seen no sign of Eirik Blacktooth!"

"Then you've not looked in the right places!" hissed the völva.

"It was *you* who has haunted us, hunted us to death! Why?"

But the little witch only returned his stare over the fire.

Haraldson's brows prowled down his forehead.

"You are in thrall to him? He has used his *trollskap* to possess you?"

Now the girl was laughing again. "No. I am performing a service to him."

"What *service* requires you murder my men?"

Her laugh vanished and she rose to her feet. "I am bringing him rest."

The old jarl felt a bitter fury bubbling inside him, like a volcanic spring.

"How is it you can bring a Draugr rest by the shedding of innocent blood?"

"Hah!" snorted the völva, "*Innocent* blood? Was your blood innocent when you slaughtered the monks at Lindesfarne? Was your blood innocent when you burned homes and murdered children? Was your blood innocent when you threw my grandmother overboard?"

The sudden silence fell like a stone.

Haraldson could only gape.

When he finally spoke, he had almost no voice left.

"Then – you are my granddaughter?"

She spat into the fire. "Ach, no! Thank the gods, you are nothing to me."

She circled the barrow now, patting the heads of his crew where they hung from the wooden posts. "Your wife – my grandmother – knew enough *galdr* to survive the cold. And she was a good enough swimmer to make it to shore. She married another man, a *good* man. When my mother was born, my grandmother taught her all her magic… and in time, my mother taught me."

Haraldson felt his mind was reeling, churning like the water at the foot of a falls.

"She cursed the *Linnorm* – made it turn on us in the storm!"

But again the witch was laughing.

"No, you old fool! You were half-crazy with the brew! The poisons bewitched you, playing tricks on your eyes! You drove your own ship onto the rocks, trying to kill a monster that was never there!"

The old jarl sagged, broken like his long-ship, a swathe of wreckage bobbing on the tide. He felt numb to the bone, as though he were sinking slowly, drowning in the dark.

Finally, with an effort, he raised his aching head and asked:

"What does Eirik Blacktooth want with us?"

Gently, she stroked his bearded cheek. "To rest in peace. Well – in pieces actually…"

She knelt beside him, looking again deeply into the old jarl's half-dead eyes.

"You still won't see it, will you?"

The words seemed to echo back to him, from a long time ago. Then he remembered: Torstein had asked him the same thing, back in the gloom of the long-hall, while the fire died slowly in the hearth. His terse answer now was the same it had been back then:

"Won't see *what?*"

She smiled sadly. "*You* – you are Eirik Blacktooth."

The sickly dizziness came rushing back, and he twisted his head to clear it while her words rang on and on in his old ears.

"*You* are the evil creature who refuses to lie in his grave. *You* are the fiend who murdered innocents, turning wives into widows and children into orphans, blighting this land with misery and ash."

The black, bony claw was pointing at him in accusation.

"You are the Draugr!"

But Haraldson was shaking his head, remembering Vidarson's words: the Draugr was trying to drive him mad, to rob him of his wits before the end.

"It's a lie!" he spat, "You're a liar!"

The girl tilted her head in sympathy. "Think, Eirik! Try to remember."

"My name is Lief Haraldson…" he argued, weakly.

She sighed. "Ja, you were born with that name… but you took another to frighten men with. Eirik Blacktooth was the name your crew gave you – black teeth from chewing on the hot coals of the fire!"

He moaned and tried to wriggle away.

"When you were buried here, the völvas put pine-needles in your feet to stop you walking again. You can still feel them, can't you?"

Not waiting for a reply, the little witch went on: "They covered your eyes with snow before carrying you into the barrow, so that you would not find your way back. They carved inscriptions into the stones to bind you in the after-life…"

Still, the old jarl struggled.

She pointed in the dark: "Your arm was torn off before you died. You used *trollskap* to seal it back in place."

"Liar!" roared the sea-captain, but she drew closer.

"Torstein was nearly right about the ravens – Huginn and Muninn: thought and memory. But they don't come to *take* your memories: they *return* them."

"No!" sobbed Haraldson, no longer sure that he was Haraldson.

"The ravens feed on you because you are *dead*! You feel cold and heavy because you are *dead*! You stink like the dead because you *are* dead! Ach, look with your eyes, old man!"

Picking a flaming branch from the fire, she held it aloft and cast enough light for him to see clearly.

His head was hung by his hair from a wooden post.

Below the neck, nothing remained.

The old jarl wailed aloud. "Witch! What have you done to me?"

"Me?" asked Gunnhild, "I have done nothing to you. You did this to yourself, years ago, with your killing and looting and your filthy brew."

She leaned against the stones of the barrow and watched him.

"If you don't believe me, ask your crew…"

The circle of severed heads raised their sorrowful eyes to him and all nodded in agreement.

"Listen to her," muttered Magnussen from the post next to his.

"It's true, Eirik!" groaned Torstein on the other side.

"We all are Draugar!" whispered Bjørnson, a little further away.

Rolf and Ulfgang hung, whining, from the next two posts.

"And it's all your fault!" hissed Vidarson.

Art by Annabelle Cross

Epilogue

Gunnhild Lashtongue left the men quarrelling in the *howe* and set off back to the long-hall, with their headless bodies stumbling behind her.

In the dawning light, she directed them as they hauled the battered hull of *Torwurm* up from the stone walls, righted it on the pebbles of the beach, and worked to patch up the holes. The beach thudded with the heart-beat of boat-building.

A few days later, as the sky brightened, they launched the long-ship again and the headless men leapt on board, each grabbing an oar and rowing away from the beach.

The girl stood in the shallow surf with her bow and enchanted arrows, watching as they pulled away… waiting until the current took them.

Then she nocked an arrow – with a little paper packet of magnesium powder swinging from the shaft – and sent it in a high arc over the waves, where it landed spitting and flaring with white fire in the wet timbers of the ship.

By the time she had emptied her quiver, the ship was ablaze.

In a short while, the smoke had drifted across the sky, and the ashes had sunk far beneath the ice.

***

On her way back across to the far side of the island where her little *knorr* was moored, Gunnhild Lashtongue passed the barrow-mound of mossy stones, and paused to listen quietly to the voices inside.

The men were still arguing: dogs barking over a fence.

"See you next winter, boys!" she sighed, "Let's do it all again."

The ravens flapped into the dark mouth of the *howe*, eager to finish feeding. Long before the last scream was over she was clambering into her *knorr*, and rowing away.

Just when her arms were beginning to tire, she felt a swelling in the water and a nudge under the hull, as the *Linnorm* slid gently beneath, and carried her back to the welcoming lights of home, softly glowing under the sea.

Glossary

aptrgangr ... "again-walker"

berserkergang ... fit of spasms and shivers

galdr ... magic cast by singing

hammask ... changing to animal form

hel-blár ... "deathly-blue"

höggspjót ... hewing spear

howe ... burial mound or barrow

hugr ... soul

jarl ... chief

kenning .... magic name

knorr ... small, flat-bottomed boat

krókspjót ... hooked spear

nár-fölr ... "corpse-white"

seidr ... clairvoyant trance

skerry ... underwater rock

Skraelings ... Inuit people

trollskap ... shape-shifting magic

Úlfhédnar ... berserker wolf-cult

völva ... witch

Here is a taste of what happens next...

Bäckahäst

Gunnhild Lashtongue Series
Book Two

Chapter One

The bog squatted between the trees, sweating like a fat brown toad. Blåheksmose, the locals called it – Blue Witch Moor. Even in the shade, the air was torpid and bloated with lazy heat; thick and whining with midges. Great fangs of dirty sunlight bit through the canopy of listless leaves and sank into the mud.

It was late July; the start of the Dog Days: the heaviest days of summer, when the air sat as still and as stodgy as porridge, clogging men's throats. Wine soured in the barrel, dogs grew savage with thirst and men lay languid in their huts; wracked with cramps, burning with fevers and frenzied with sunstroke. The brackish bog-water rose in writhing ropes of vapour, and the moisture shrank slowly into the moss and peat.

Far out across the mire, something stirred.

A tiny gang of bubbles slid up against the filthy skin of the bog and glooped their last stinking breath into the sun-baked haze.

Shortly after, something followed them: some mud-plastered, crawling creature, thrashing its way up from under a twisted mass of sticks. Groping its way over the surface, it caught a branch and began drawing itself up from the sucking muck. For a torturous quarter hour or more, it slapped and splatted across the bog, seeking the edge where the moss grew firmer over the roots of the stunted trees.

Finally it stood, and surveyed its reflection in the murky water: a matted tangle of hair, knotted like filthy rope; coppery body paint, still gleaming on its shoulders under a cake of muck; a weary face, wrinkled and stained black from the peaty bog. Over all of this was an eerie, pale green paste, dripping thickly down its arms and legs.

The bogman wondered briefly whether it had been his stag night: his head throbbed terribly; his throat was sore and stuffed with mud; his arms and legs felt as rubbery and useless as green twigs. His stomach heaved suddenly and he retched up several mouthfuls of dark bog water. Skeletal leaves caught in his teeth and his eyes streamed through a crust of grit. He was pretty sure it had to have been his stag night.

His clothes were gone – a short time later, he found them neatly folded but sodden with mud, wedged under the same woven hurdle that had been used to flatten him down in the bog. Throwing the dripping garments over a branch in the sun, he sat on a stump and waited for them to dry.

Shielding his eyes with one hand, he tried to peer across to the far edges of the sprawling swamp that surrounded him on all sides. His eyes felt like two weak and starving moles that had finally surfaced after too long under the ground. Knives of sunlight flashed on the black puddles and sliced through his eyelids, setting his skull ringing and his guts squirming again. Through the blinding glare and the buzzing insects, he could just make out a varp next to him on the edge of the bog: a small pile of stones, left by travellers to mark their passing. In keeping with the ancient custom, he added his own stone to the stack.

When his clothes had dried, he tugged them on; stiff and scratchy and flaking with dirt. All the while, he was still trawling through his aching brain for any details of the night before. He was having difficulty recalling even his own name. However, as he pushed his kitten-weak arms through the sleeves, he realised he had bigger problems. His left hand was missing...

About the Author

Geoff Hill grew up in the Cotswolds and trained as a teacher in Aberystwyth, before settling in Wiltshire and teaching at a number of schools. He wrote Draugr for his 2015 class while they were studying the Vikings. He lives near Bath with his wife and son and Millie the cat.

And if you want to meet a Viking in real life do get in touch with Hrothgar the Viking!

Bring the sagas to life with Hrothgar the Viking. Over 25 years visiting schools in England and Wales.
Email: hrothgar@manaraefan.co.uk
Twitter: @VikingHrothgar
Phone: 07979513140

Lightning Source UK Ltd.
Milton Keynes UK
UKHW020841060220
358266UK00008B/109